HILLSBORO PUBLIC LIBRARIES
Hillsboro, OR
Member of Washington County
COOPERATIVE LIBRARY SERVICES

D0463020

Mr. King's Things

For Rose and Zoe, and for all Cape Farewell Climate Change champions — G.C.

Text and illustrations © 2012 Geneviève Côté

All rights reserved. No part of this publication may be reproduced, stored in a retrieval system or transmitted, in any form or by any means, without the prior written permission of Kids Can Press Ltd. or, in case of photocopying or other reprographic copying, a license from The Canadian Copyright Licensing Agency (Access Copyright). For an Access Copyright license, visit www.accesscopyright.ca or call toll free to 1-800-893-5777.

Kids Can Press acknowledges the financial support of the Government of Ontario, through the Ontario Media Development Corporation's Ontario Book Initiative; the Ontario Arts Council; the Canada Council for the Arts; and the Government of Canada, through the BPIDP, for our publishing activity.

Published in Canada by
Kids Can Press Ltd.
25 Dockside Drive
Toronto, ON M5A 0B5

Published in the U.S. by
Kids Can Press Ltd.
2250 Military Road
Tonawanda, NY 14150

www.kidscanpress.com

Kids Can Press is a *Corus*™ Entertainment company

The artwork in this book was rendered in multi-media.
The text is set in Futura Book.

Edited by Tara Walker and Sheila Barry
Designed by Karen Powers

This book is smyth sewn casebound.
Manufactured in China, in 3/2012, through
Asia Pacific Offset, 3/F, New factory (No.12),
Jing Yi Industrial Center, Tian Bei Estate, Fu Ming
Community, Guan Lan, Bao An, Shenzhen, China

CM 12 0 9 8 7 6 5 4 3 2 1

FSC
www.fsc.org
MIX
Paper from
responsible sources
FSC® C012521

Library and Archives Canada Cataloguing in Publication

Côté, Geneviève, 1964–

　　Mr. King's things / written and illustrated by Geneviève Côté.

ISBN 978-1-55453-700-6   5037 3249   12/12

　　I. Title.

PS8605.O8738M57 2012　　　jC813'.6　　　C2011-907939-9

Geneviève Côté

Mr. King's Things

HILLSBORO PUBLIC LIBRARIES
Member of Washington County
COOPERATIVE LIBRARY SERVICES

KIDS CAN PRESS

Mr. King likes new things.
LOTS of new things.

As soon as one of his things becomes
the tiniest bit old, he tosses it into the
nearby pond and replaces it with a new
one. The pond isn't big, but it can
hold a LOT. And nothing ever shows
except a few ripples.

When he isn't buying new things or tossing
old things, Mr. King goes fishing.

There aren't many fish, but Mr. King doesn't mind. He just likes to lie in the sun.

But this morning, Mr. King is almost rocked out of his boat by a sudden tug.

"Uh-oh! This must be a really BIG fish!"

He pulls on his line ...

...and up comes the scariest-looking thing
Mr. King has **EVER** seen!

"HELP! A MONSTER!!"

Mr. King rows away as fast as he can, but the monster is hooked to his line and it follows him closely.

It follows him right onto the shore!
The minute his boat lands, Mr. King runs for
cover and sits tight, eyes shut, hands on ears.

His friends come rushing
to the pond. Mr. King is
nowhere to be seen.

"What was all the noise?"

"Is the circus in town?"

Mr. King's friends look around for clues, and find a BIG pile of things jumbled on the shore.

"A jumble sale!" cries Harriet. "I LOVE jumble sales!"

"I could use this ladder," says Bert. "I'm not very good at climbing trees."

"Oooh, what a lovely house!" say Skit and Skat.

"Let me fix this umbrella for you, Harriet," offers Old Jim Elk.

"Now I'll have enough chairs to seat my whole family!" exclaims P.J.

"And I'll take a table for two," says Tex.

Mr. King is still hiding, wondering where the monster is. When he peeks out to look, he spots his friends standing by the pond! "OH NO!"

He runs over to warn them.

"WATCH OUT! There's a MONSTER over there. WATCH OUT!"

Mr. King stops short. THE MONSTER IS GONE!

"Look!" says Skit. "We found a table,
a teapot, six chairs, a tuba..."

"...and we saved some nice things
for you!" says Skat.

Mr. King turns quite red.
"Uh-oh," he says, "these are my old things!"

He picks up a few pieces thoughtfully.
"Hmm ... I have an idea!" he announces,
and he sets to work.

Everyone is thrilled with Mr. King's inventions!
He has made a flower-kite, a fish-carousel, a floating
fountain, a colorful surfboard and a ferryboat for two.

Mr. King likes to turn OLD things into NEW!

HILLSBORO PUBLIC LIBRARIES
Hillsboro, OR
Member of Washington County
COOPERATIVE LIBRARY SERVICES